Cool Moves

Story by Chris McTrustry
Illustrations by Chantal Stewart

Contents

Chapter 1

The Semi-final

It was a tense moment in the semi-final of the chess tournament between Melody Hope and Tara Vale. It was Tara's move and all eyes were upon her. Grinning, Tara pushed her long, golden hair behind her dainty ears and confidently reached for her one remaining knight.

"Let's see you get out of this," she said to Melody, plunking the knight down firmly. "It's your move, Cool Moves."

"That's your move?" Melody asked. She eased a little closer to the table and leaned over the board.

"Yes," Tara smiled. "Oh, I believe they call that 'check'."

"And this," Melody said, pinching her queen by the crown and sliding it toward Tara's freshly moved knight, "is what they call 'checkmate'." She replaced Tara's knight with her queen.

"What?" Tara screeched. "But you — but that's...!" She looked at the board, then glared at Melody. "You, you... tricked me!" Tara pushed back her chair and stormed away from the table.

"Gee, she's a good sport," said Melody's best friend, Carlo Santini. He looked down at Melody and grinned. "I'm really glad you beat her. If Tara had got into the final she would have gone on and on — and on — about it."

Melody shrugged. "She played all right. She just got a little overconfident."

Melody had started to pack up her chess pieces when the referee, a squat middle-aged man with large round glasses, came over.

"I hear you had a good win," he said, slowly and very loudly. "Congratulations."

Melody winced and swapped an amused look with Carlo. "Thanks," she said.

"We meet back here tomorrow for the final," the referee continued loudly, gesturing at the room. "Ten o'clock. Okay?"

"Okay," Melody said, very slowly.

The referee smiled. "Good," he shouted.

Carlo couldn't take anymore. "She can't use her *legs!*" he pointed out. "But her *ears* are fine. She can hear perfectly."

The referee blushed. "Pardon me," he said, realizing his mistake.

"That's okay," Melody said good-naturedly. "Who's my opponent?"

"A young man by the name of Iggie Pike," the referee said.

"Iggie?" Carlo said. "No way!"

"Oh, yes," the referee said. "He has played some very good games."

Chapter 2

The Prize

"Iggie Pike plays chess?" Carlo muttered as he and Melody made their way home. "Iggie plays chess?"

"That's the three-hundredth time you've said that," Melody chuckled.

"But it doesn't make sense," Carlo said. "I bet he can't even spell chess. And I'm sure he can't play it."

"Well, he's my opponent and I'll beat him," Melody said.

"Yeah," said Carlo. "And win fifty dollars for first place! Are you still going to surprise your mom with a present?"

"Oh, yes." Melody twisted around in her chair. "You won't tell her, will you?"

"Of course not." Carlo sighed. "It's too bad she had to work today and missed you thrashing Miss Hoity-Toity Tara."

"She always has to work," Melody said sadly. "She's been so busy ever since we moved here... " Her voice trailed off.

Melody and her mom had moved to Daletown only six months earlier. Melody's mom had been promoted to bank manager, and had been working long hours every day to try to get on top of the job.

Some of the kids were a bit shy about approaching Melody when she started at her new school. There weren't any other kids in wheelchairs at the school and they weren't sure what to do. But Melody was very confident and cheerful and eventually the other kids no longer noticed her disability.

Melody was a real whiz in her wheelchair and found herself dubbed with the nickname "Cool Moves." It bugged Carlo, her best friend, but Melody secretly thought her new nickname was cool.

Chapter 3

A Bet

"Well, well," said a gruff voice from behind the two friends. "If it isn't Cool Moves and her snail power motor!"

Carlo whirled around. "Iggie! Why don't you go and crawl back under your rock!"

"Be nice, Santini," Iggie growled.

Carlo glared at Iggie. "So how come you can play chess? All you do is ride your skateboard and play games on your computer."

"Computers are educational," Iggie said.

Carlo laughed. "Blasting aliens is educational?"

Iggie smiled menacingly. "Seeing you're so curious, I'll tell you how I learned to play chess," he said. "I've got this cool chess game on my computer. And when you take a piece... " — he smacked a fist into the palm of his other hand — "Whammo! It gets its head cut off by the attacking piece. It's awesome."

Then Iggie shrugged. "I got sick of being dumped on all the time, so I figured out how to play — properly."

"Too much," Carlo muttered.

"So, Cool Moves, are you looking forward to the final?" asked Iggie.

"I'm looking forward to winning," Melody said confidently.

Carlo cheered.

"First prize is fifty dollars. Second is only ten. I've got a deal for you," Iggie said.

"Yeah?" said Melody.

"The winner gets the lot. Sixty dollars. Nothing for losers — as it should be."

"Don't do it, Melody," Carlo warned.

Melody thrust out her hand. "You've got a bet, Iggie," she said. "The winner gets the lot."

Chapter 4

The Appointment

Early the next morning, Carlo stopped by Melody's apartment.

"Oh, Carlo! I'm glad you're on time!" said Mrs. Hope, frantically waving Carlo inside. "I've been called into work early this morning."

"But that means you'll miss the chess final!" Carlo said.

"Yes, but I just have to go," Mrs. Hope replied sadly. "And I won't be able to drive Melody to her physical therapy appointment either."

"Now?" Carlo squeaked. "Today? This morning? But... but..."

"I know how important the chess final is, Carlo. Really I do. And you don't know how disappointed I am to miss it," Mrs. Hope shrugged wearily. "But it's also very important that Melody receives her treatment. I've called for a special taxi to take you two to the physical therapy clinic, but I'm afraid they are all booked up for the remainder of the day. You'll have to make your own way to the school afterward. I'm sorry, but it's the best I can do."

"Don't worry, Mrs. Hope, we'll be all right," Carlo said. "And you're right, we've got to think of Melody."

Mrs. Hope smiled. "Thank you, Carlo. You're a good friend."

Moments later, a glum-faced Melody wheeled herself into the apartment's small living room. "I guess Mom told you her plan," she muttered.

"Don't worry," Carlo said, trying to stay positive. "We'll get to the final in plenty of time."

"The taxi will be here very soon, Melody," said Mrs. Hope, gathering up her purse and keys. She gave Melody a quick kiss goodbye — and an extra kiss for luck — and hurried off to work.

Thankfully, the taxi was on time, and it dropped Melody and Carlo outside the physical therapy clinic.

"Plenty of time," Carlo said, checking his watch after he had helped Melody out of the taxi. "Loads of time. Tons of time. You want time, we've got it!"

"Well then, let's not hang around, eh?" Melody urged.

"Good idea," Carlo said, hurrying along next to Melody's wheelchair. "Prepare to engage engine in Warp Factor One!"

But suddenly Carlo hesitated and placed his hand on Melody's shoulder.

"What's up?" asked Melody. "My engine hasn't stalled."

"No," Carlo muttered. "But maybe we should put it into reverse." He pointed down the street. "Do you see who I see?"

Iggie Pike stood by a lamppost, grinning at them.

Melody took a deep breath. "If this is pre-match harassment, I can handle it," she said.

"What are you doing here, Iggie?" Carlo said, as they drew near.

"My mom's shopping and it's my turn to help her."

"Looks like you're really helping," Carlo smirked.

"You're not very funny, Santini," Iggie said. "So, what are you two doing here?"

"I've got a physical therapy appointment," replied Melody.

Iggie smiled, as if he'd just thought of something very funny.

"Good idea. I'd hate to see you cramp up during the final, Cool Moves," he said. "I want some decent opposition."

"We'll see if you're still bragging after the final," Carlo grunted.

"Oh, I think I will be," Iggie said. "You can bet on it."

Chapter 5

Disaster

Mr. Green, the therapist, ran the clinic by himself. He smiled as Carlo and Melody came into his small, congested waiting room.

"Ah, Madam, Sir," he said in an awful French accent. "Your table is ready."

"Terrific," Melody murmured.

Mr. Green led Melody and Carlo into an even smaller room. There was a desk, a chair, and a long treatment table. He gently eased Melody onto the treatment table then gestured at the small room, nodding at Melody's wheelchair.

"As you can see, there's barely enough room to turn around in here," he said. "Carlo, could you please park Melody's chair out in the hallway? You can wait in the waiting room."

"Okay," Carlo said.

The therapy session eased a lot of tension Melody wasn't even aware of. When it was over, Mr. Green put his head around the door to the waiting room.

"Okay, Carlo, we've finished. Send in the young lady's chariot."

With a grin, Carlo hurried out to the hallway. Then, with a scream, he rushed back through the waiting room into the treatment room.

"It's gone!" he said.

"What's gone?" said a puzzled Mr. Green.

"Melody's chair," Carlo said in a hollow voice. "It's... gone."

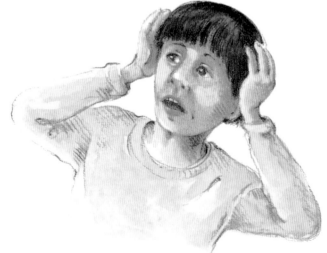

Chapter 6

Never Say Never

"No prizes for guessing who's taken it," Melody said.

"That's sabotage!" exclaimed Carlo. "Iggie's making sure he wins the final! By hook or by crook!"

"I'll call Mom," Melody said. "Maybe she can pick us up."

Mr. Green placed the phone on the end of the treatment table. "Help yourself," he offered.

"Thanks," said a grateful Melody. But after a short conversation, Melody reported that her mom couldn't get away from work for at least another hour.

"But the chess final starts in twenty-five minutes!" Carlo wailed. He explained the situation to Mr. Green.

"I'd drive you there myself," Mr. Green said. "But I've got patients to see."

"That's okay," said Melody, as Mr. Green bustled out of the room.

"No, it's not," Carlo replied. "We're never going to make it." He smacked a fist into his palm.

Melody shook her head. "Never say never, Carlo," she said defiantly.

"Okay," he said. "We'll *probably* never make it on time. That Iggie Pike. I could just... just... just... I don't know what I could do, but it would NOT be pleasant!"

"Okay, okay," said Melody. "But before we can exact revenge, we have to get to the final. Do you have any suggestions?"

Carlo bit his bottom lip. After thirty seconds of "umming" and "ahhing," he shook his head. "Nothing. Sorry."

"What about your mom?" Melody suggested. "Would she be able to pick us up?"

"Normally, yes," explained Carlo. "But today she's taken my grandmother to visit her sister in the hospital."

"Then we need another form of transportation," Melody said.

"I've got my skateboard in my bag. Maybe I could take you on that," Carlo suggested.

"No way!" laughed Melody. "We'd both end up in wheelchairs that way."

Mr. Green returned to the treatment room. "I'm sorry, kids. I tried to order a taxi, but they're all booked and I've got to see my next patient. I can make Melody comfortable out in the waiting room if you like, until her mom can come. It's a pity about the chess final, but I don't think I can do anything for you."

"You haven't got a spare wheelchair, have you, Mr. Green?" asked Melody.

"No, I haven't any room to keep equipment, as you can see," said Mr. Green. "But... hang on... there might be something in the storeroom outside. Look, here's the key, Carlo. My next patient is waiting. I really can't help you now, but you can go out and have a look. Down the hall, out the back door, and on the left. You can use anything you find. Mind your step — there's lots of junk out there."

"Thanks, Mr. Green. Melody, I'll be as quick as I can." Carlo raced off down the hallway.

Mr. Green turned to Melody. "Come on, I'll set you up in the waiting room."

Ten minutes later, Carlo burst in the door with a battered old shopping cart. "There wasn't a wheelchair, Melody, but look what I found outside," he said. "It rattles and it's dusty and wobbly, but it goes — just. Here, I'll help you in. Hold on for the ride of your life."

Chapter 7

The Final

"Hello, Iggie."

Iggie turned, grinning, but his smile quickly slipped away when he realized it was Melody who had greeted him. "You!"

"Of course it's me," Melody said. "We do have a final to play. Remember?"

"I, er... er... er," Iggie stammered. "Umm... er..."

"I agree wholeheartedly," Melody said, smiling broadly as Carlo wheeled her up to the chess table. "Let's play."

"But you can't play in that!" Iggie shrieked.

The referee and his assistant — and a flurry of papers, clipboards, and flapping cardigans — bustled over. "What's happening over here? What's this, Melody? Iggie? Explain yourselves, please."

Melody explained what had happened. The referee was furious. Iggie turned bright red. Carlo helped Melody from the shopping cart, after Iggy miraculously 'found' Melody's wheelchair in the parking lot outside.

The final began.

Ten minutes into the match, Iggie was in serious trouble. Melody had him in 'check.' The match was all but over.

It was Melody's turn. She snatched up her queen, then eye-balled Iggie. "Do you remember our bet?" she asked.

A tight-lipped Iggie gulped, then nodded.

"I don't," Melody said.

"Huh?" The snarl melted away from Iggie's face. He stared at Melody, puzzled.

"You deserve a reward for getting to the final. You've earned it," Melody said softly. "But what you did to me, it... it... it..."

"Stinks!" Carlo interjected. "Stick to the bet, Melody."

Melody shook her head. "No," she said, suddenly close to tears. "That would make me just as mean as Iggie."

Iggie looked at Melody for a long time. Then he nodded.

Melody slowly lowered her queen and knocked over Iggie's king.

"Checkmate," Iggie said, softly. "You win."